Happy Christmas, Little Bear

For Sunshine Girl — MA
For Oscar and Tia. The two special little people in my life–AS

Little Hare Books
8/21 Mary Street, Surry Hills
NSW 2010 AUSTRALIA

www.littleharebooks.com

National Library of Australia
Cataloguing-in-Publication entry

Allum, Margaret.
Happy Christmas, Little Bear / Margaret Allum :
illustrator, Angela Swan.
9781921541247 (hbk.)
For pre-school age.
Gifts--Juvenile fiction.
Christmas stories.
Bears--Juvenile fiction.
A823.4

Designed by Vida and Luke Kelly
Produced by Pica Digital
Printed in China through Phoenix Offset

5 4 3 2 1

Happy Christmas, Little Bear

Margaret Allum ★ Angela Swan

LITTLE HARE

www.littleharebooks.com

Little Bear's Christmas list was so long that it covered two pieces of paper.

'I'm not sure if Santa can manage all that,' said Mummy Bear.

'Yes he can,' said Little Bear, 'or it won't be a happy Christmas.'

'Perhaps you can make it shorter,' said Daddy Bear.

'No, I won't,' said Little Bear, and he ran off to hide under the stairs.

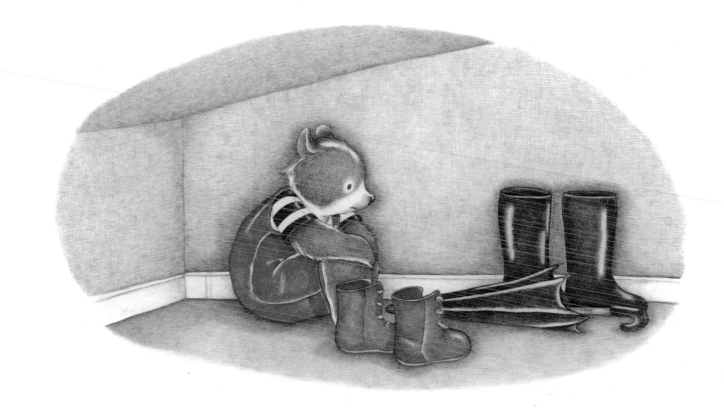

'You must choose your favourite thing,' said Mummy Bear.

'I won't choose,' shouted Little Bear. 'I want it all!'

'Then Santa will have to choose for you,' said Daddy Bear.

'I don't want Santa to choose!' yelled Little Bear,
and he ran off to hide behind the sofa.

That evening Daddy Bear asked,
'Are you ready to choose, Little Bear?'

'I want the skateboard, the hobbyhorse, the pogo stick and the tricycle,'
said Little Bear. 'I want everything!'

'Your presents have to share the space in Santa's sack,'
said Daddy Bear. 'Santa may not have room.'

'If I have to share,' yelled Little Bear,
'it won't be a happy Christmas!'
And he hid his head under his blanket.

When Christmas came, Little Bear saw many presents under the tree.
He saw a long one, and a big one, and a thin one.
But Little Bear wasn't allowed to touch them.

He had to wait for his
uncle to arrive.

Then he had to wait for his aunt
and his cousins to arrive.

Then he had to wait for his
grandma to arrive.

At last everyone was there.

'Now I can open all the presents that Santa has brought me,'
said Little Bear.

The first one was something long, like a skateboard.
But it wasn't for Little Bear. It was for Cousin Panda.

The next one was something big, like a hobbyhorse.
But it wasn't for Little Bear. It was for Cousin Grizzly.

The last one was something thin, like a pogo stick.
But it wasn't for Little Bear. It was for Cousin Fuzzy.

'Where's my present?' shouted Little Bear.

'Happy Christmas,' said Mummy Bear,
as she handed Little Bear something square
and flat and white.

Little Bear had never seen such a square present.
Or such a flat present. Or such a white present.
It wasn't a proper present at all.

He didn't even bother to open it.
Instead he stuffed it in his pocket
and ran away to hide under the kitchen table.

While Little Bear was under the table, Cousin Panda
tried to ride his new skateboard. He kept falling off.

Little Bear crawled out to watch.

Cousin Grizzly tried to ride her new hobbyhorse.
But she couldn't climb on.

Little Bear crept along the hall.

Cousin Fuzzy tried to ride his new pogo stick.
But it wouldn't bounce.

Little Bear peeped into the parlour.

'I'll help you steady your skateboard,
Cousin Panda,' said Little Bear.

Cousin Panda had so much fun
that he rolled and rolled,
all around the room.

'I'll help you onto your hobbyhorse,'
said Little Bear to Cousin Grizzly.

Cousin Grizzly had so much fun
that she galloped and galloped,
up and down the hall.

'I'll help you bounce your pogo stick, Cousin Fuzzy,'
said Little Bear.

Cousin Fuzzy had so much fun that he
bounced and bounced, all the way to the kitchen.

Little Bear ran back and forth, helping his cousins with their galloping, their rolling and their bouncing.

He had so much fun that he forgot all about his present.

'Have you forgotten something, Little Bear?' said Daddy Bear.

Little Bear remembered his square, flat, white present.
He took it out of his pocket. He opened it.
Inside it were the words, 'Look under the stairs.'

Little Bear looked under the stairs. In the darkness was a present. It was something lumpy, like a tricycle. And it was for him!

Grizzly and Panda and Fuzzy climbed on board,
and Little Bear pedalled and pedalled them ...

all around the house.

Happy Christmas, Little Bear!